How Bugs and Plants Live Together

I0799346

Yvonne Misztal

INFOMAX COMMON CORE READERS

Rosen Classroom™

New York

Published in 2014 by The Rosen Publishing Group, Inc.
29 East 21st Street, New York, NY 10010

Book Design: Michael J. Flynn

Photo Credits: Cover Anny Chan/Shutterstock.com; p. 5 momopixs/Shutterstock.com; p. 7 Klagyivik Viktor/Shutterstock.com; p. 9 (background) Tanee/Shutterstock.com; p. 9 (flower) Dreamy Girl/Shutterstock.com; p. 9 (bee) Analia26/Shutterstock.com; p. 11 Evgeny Parushin/Shutterstock.com; p. 13 Christian Musat/Shutterstock.com; p. 15 (main) Roger Meerts/Shutterstock.com; p. 15 (inset) chinahbzyg/Shutterstock.com; p. 17 Roman Prokhorov/Shutterstock.com; p. 19 kurt_G/Shutterstock.com; p. 21 Henrik Larsson/Shutterstock.com; p. 22 fotorich01/Shutterstock.com.

ISBN: 978-1-4777-2446-0
6-pack ISBN: 978-1-4777-2447-7

Manufactured in the United States of America

CPSIA Compliance Information: Batch #CS13RC: For further information contact Rosen Publishing, New York, New York at 1-800-237-9932.

Contents

Different Relationships

Have you ever seen a bee flying around a flower or a ladybug crawling on a leaf? Bugs and plants have very special relationships, or connections, between them. Certain bugs and plants enjoy the same kinds of weather and live well together.

When plants and bugs use each other to stay alive, both sides benefit, or gain something. There are special relationships even in your backyard!

The next time you see a plant, look closely to see what kinds of critters are near it.

What's Pollination?

Good relationships are about giving and taking, which happens during pollination. That's when a bug, such as a bee or butterfly, carries **pollen** from one flower to another. Pollen allows flowers to make new seeds.

Pollination is a good example of giving and taking. The bees give pollen to plants and take food from them. Plants give food to the bees and take pollen from them.

The yellow powder on the bee's legs is pollen.

Let's follow a bee during pollination! First, the bee finds a flower. There is tasty nectar—a sweet juice—in the flowers. Next, the bee crawls inside and takes the nectar to feed the other bees in its hive.

As the bee takes the nectar, it also gets pollen on its legs. The bee carries the pollen to the next flower. It doesn't even do this on purpose!

Bees have very important jobs to do!

A Bee's Job

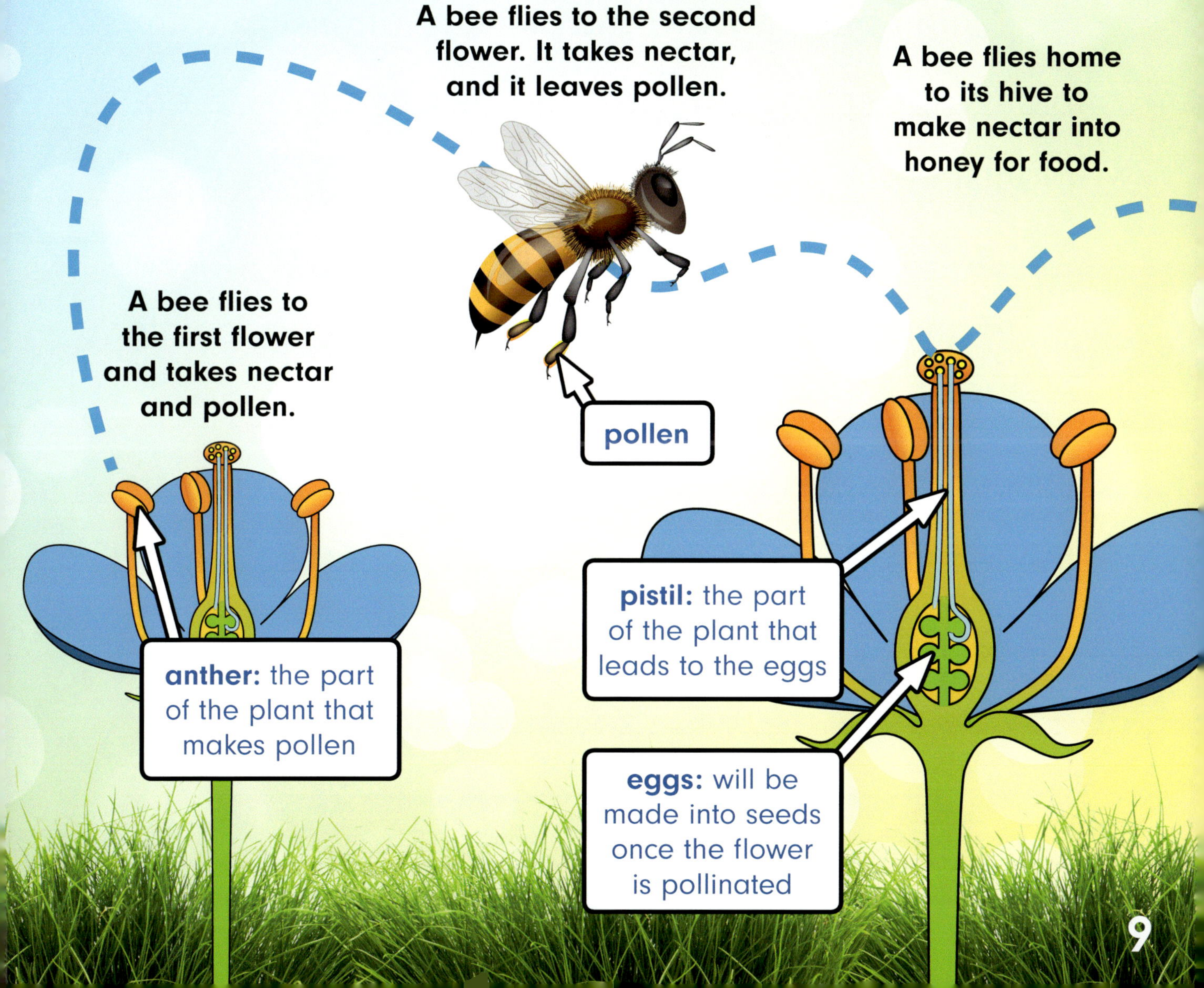
A bee flies to the second flower. It takes nectar, and it leaves pollen.
A bee flies home to its hive to make nectar into honey for food.
A bee flies to the first flower and takes nectar and pollen.
pollen
pistil: the part of the plant that leads to the eggs
anther: the part of the plant that makes pollen
eggs: will be made into seeds once the flower is pollinated

Bad Bugs

When bugs have a **parasitic** relationship with plants, they're called pests. Many pests love to eat plants. Pests include aphids and grasshoppers. Some moths and caterpillars are pests, too.

Aphids are tiny bugs that use their long, pointed mouthparts to break into plants and drink their juices. They attack the soft parts of a plant, such as the leaves. They can also spread sicknesses that kill the plants.

There are many different kinds of aphids, and they're present on most plants.

Keeping Safe

Many bugs help **protect** plants from pests. Some of these good bugs are ladybugs, lacewings, and hoverflies.

Ladybugs are great for controlling pests. They lay their eggs on leaves. After their **larvae** break out of their eggs, they eat a lot of aphids! Grown-up ladybugs like to eat aphids, too, but they don't eat as many as the larvae do.

Ladybug larvae can eat 40 aphids in an hour and still be hungry!

Lacewings are little bugs that are green or brown and have big wings. They lay small white eggs on the ends of white threads. Their larvae look like tiny alligators and love to eat aphids.

Lacewings are sometimes called "aphid lions." Farmers and gardeners can buy lacewing larvae to keep pests under control. This is better than using unnatural sprays to keep pests away.

Lacewings are nature's way of keeping pest problems under control.

lacewing larva

Have you ever seen tiny bees that **hover** over plants and then fly quickly away? They might not be bees at all! Hoverflies are flies that look like tiny bees. They're friendly to people, and good for plants.

Hoverfly maggots, or larvae without legs, feed on many leaf pests. Their maggots come in many different colors, such as green, yellow, orange, and white.

Hoverflies look like tiny bees, but they're actually flies. Don't worry—they don't sting!

Plants protect bugs, too. As we've seen, plants are great places to lay eggs. The undersides of leaves are protected from bad weather, such as wind and rain. This keeps eggs safe.

Adult bugs live and hide in plants. At night, some butterflies hold on to the underside of a leaf to sleep. Many bugs live inside plants, such as trees. Some ants and bees make homes high up in trees to stay safe from enemies.

Leaves are good places for bugs to stay when it's raining!

Helpful Ants

Many carpenter ants make their homes in logs. It's easy for them to chew away the wood and make tunnels to live in. In nature, this is a very important relationship.

Logs are dead trees, so they're plants that aren't alive anymore. By chewing through them, ants help the trees to decompose, or break down. The **nutrients** from decomposed plants become part of the soil. Living plants use the nutrients to grow.

Helping plants decompose is a very important job in nature.

In Your Garden

Bugs are more than just creepy-crawly critters. They serve important purposes in nature. If you have a garden, look around to see how the plants and bugs are living together. Do your plants have yellowing leaves or black spots on them? If so, you may have pests. Do your plants have healthy green leaves and pretty flowers? If so, then your plants and bugs are working together as a team!

Glossary

hover (HUH-vuhr) To float in the air without moving around much.

larvae (LAHR-vee) Insects after they come out of their eggs and before they become adults.

nutrient (NOO-tree-uhnt) Something that helps people, animals, and plants live and grow.

parasitic (pehr-uh-SIH-tihk) Having to do with a connection between two living things that benefits one and hurts the other.

pollen (PAH-luhn) The yellow dust a flowering plant makes.

protect (pruh-TEHKT) To keep safe.

Index